THIS CANDLEWICK BOOK BELONGS TO:

_____

_____

_____

_____

Copyright © 1992 by Catherine and Laurence Anholt

First U.S. paperback edition 1994
First published in Great Britain in 1992 by Walker Books Ltd., London.

Library of Congress Cataloging-in-Publication Data

Anholt, Catherine
The twins two by two/Catherine and Laurence Anholt.–1st U.S. ed.
"First published in Great Britain in 1992 by Walker Books Ltd., London"—T.p. verso.
Summary: Inspired by a bedtime story about Noah's ark, twins Minnie and Max become
pairs of crocodiles, elephants, bats, and other animals as they prepare for bed.
ISBN 1-56402-041-X (hardcover)—ISBN 1-56402-397-4 (paperback)
[1. Bedtime—Fiction. 2. Twins—Fiction. 3. Animals—Fiction.]
I. Anholt, Laurence. II. Title. III. Title: Twins 2 by 2.
PZ7.A5863Tw 1992
[E]–dc20   91-28210
2 4 6 8 10 9 7 5 3 1

Printed in Hong Kong

The pictures in this book were done in watercolor and ink.

Candlewick Press
2067 Massachusetts Avenue
Cambridge, Massachusetts 02140

THE TWINS
TWO BY TWO

Catherine and Laurence Anholt

CANDLEWICK PRESS
CAMBRIDGE, MASSACHUSETTS

Minnie and Max were having a bedtime story. It was about Noah's ark and all the animals.

"Now it's off to bed two by two," said Mommy.

On the stairs, the twins were tigers...

and in the bathroom, they splashed like crocodiles.

"You sound like two noisy elephants," said Mommy when she came up.

"We're not elephants.
  We're two little monkeys,"
  said Minnie.

"You certainly are," said
Mommy, tucking them
into bed.

In the dark, the twins were
two bats flying.

Then they jumped around
like kangaroos.

There was so much noise
that Daddy came up.
But where were the twins?

"We're two little bears,"
said a voice from under
the blankets.

Daddy put one little bear
back in his own bed.

But soon Minnie heard
Max crying.

"There's a lion under my
bed," he sniffed.

Minnie was very brave.
She looked under Max's
bed. It wasn't a lion.

It was Ginger!

The twins curled up together and closed their eyes.

"We're two little mice," they whispered – then fell fast asleep.

CATHERINE AND LAURENCE ANHOLT met in art school. They have since collaborated on several books, including *Kids, Here Come the Babies*, and *Toddlers*. "All our ideas," says Catherine, "spring from our own family experiences, and we test out all our ideas on our three children. The twins in *Two by Two* are our own twins, Maddie and Tom." The Anholts have also teamed up to create *Come Back, Jack*.